# Chapter One

When Jimjams woke up on Thursday morning, he found a note on the end of his bed:

WE'VE GOT YOUR RAT. PAY US £1,000,000 (ONE MILLION POUNDS) OR WE'LL SET THE CAT ON HIM.

Jimjams ran to Skintail's cage. The door was wide open and there was no sign of Skintail.

"Skintail!" wailed Jimjams. "How am I going to get hold of one million pounds?"

It was then that he saw
a little brown oblong on
the floor, like those
chocolate bits on cakes. One
metre away was another one, and yet
another just outside his bedroom door.

"Oh, Skintail," cried Jimjams. "What a
clever rat you are. You've left a trail of
droppings for me to follow!"

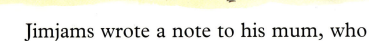

Jimjams wrote a note to his mum, who
was still asleep:

# Jimjams and the Ratnappers

*Illustrated by Scoular Anderson*

He trod his way carefully alongside the trail of droppings. Twenty-five droppings further on, the trail stopped. Jimjams had reached the end of next door's garden.

"Where to now?" wailed Jimjams. "Poor Skintail must have run out of droppings."

Just at that moment, next door's door opened and out came Chinwag, Jimjams' talkative friend.

"What's up, Jimjams?" she asked.

"Skintail's been ratnapped.

If I don't hand over
one million pounds,
a cat will have him
for supper."

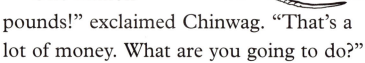

"One million
pounds!" exclaimed Chinwag. "That's a
lot of money. What are you going to do?"

"I'll have to find Skintail before it's too
late," said Jimjams. "He left a trail of
droppings, but they ran out just here."

Chinwag jumped up and down
excitedly. "I saw them! I saw them!"
she yelled.

"Saw the droppings?" said Jimjams.

"No, silly," giggled Chinwag. "Saw the men who took Skintail. Two of them."

Chinwag began to tell how she hadn't been able to sleep, how she had looked out of her window at the full moon, and how she had seen two suspicious-looking men hurrying past her house. They had both been wearing berets.

"They must be French!" said Jimjams.
"Poor Skintail could be in France by
now!"

"Let's go then," said Chinwag.

"Go where?"

"To France, of course!"

# Chapter Two

Chinwag disappeared indoors and reappeared with a duffel bag over her shoulder, wearing her Brownie hat, and looking at a book called *Tracks and Signs*. She bent down to study the little brown droppings on the ground.

"You're right," she said, importantly. "These are definitely rat droppings. I know because I'm a Brownie. Follow me, Jimjams."

She marched off
down the road,
Jimjams hurrying after
her. A number 65 bus
going to Dover came
along and they
hopped on. On the
bus Chinwag noticed
a small article in a
newspaper someone
had left behind.

RATNAPPERS STRIKE AGAIN!

"Look, Jimjams, look!"

**RATNAPPERS STRIKE AGAIN**

A gang of Ratnappers is stealing pet rats and demanding money for their return. The gang escape with the rats across the English Channel. Police have so far failed to catch the gang but they are trying very hard.

"You were right, Chinwag. But how are we going to get across the Channel?" groaned Jimjams.

"We'll swim," said Chinwag.

"Swim!" yelled Jimjams. "It's miles!"

"We'll take it slowly," said Chinwag.

13

They jumped off the bus at
the docks and walked to
the water's edge. Chinwag
searched in her duffel bag
and pulled out two packets of lard.

"Here," she said, "cover yourself in this.
It'll stop you getting cold. I know, because
I'm a Brownie."

"Yuck!" said Jimjams. "It's all slimy."
"Let's go," said Chinwag.
They walked into the freezing cold sea
and set off in a slow crawl. After one mile
Jimjams could go no further.

"It's no good, Chinwag," he said. "France is too far."

"Wait a minute," said Chinwag. "What's that over there?"

Jimjams saw an old door floating on the sea.

"We could use it as a raft," said Chinwag.

They swam over to it, scrambled on and started to paddle with their hands. Half an hour later, they passed a swimmer coming in the other direction.

"Are we nearly in France?" asked Chinwag.

"Over there, I think," said the swimmer. "Or is it over there? Or it might be over there. Can't stop any longer. Bye."

Jimjams was about to despair, when he looked over the side of the raft and saw a tiny brown object bobbing in the water. Then he saw another, and another.

"Chinwag," he yelled excitedly. "I've found some droppings. Skintail must have been here. Paddle this way."

Jimjams and Chinwag followed a trail of thirty-one droppings before it ran out.

"That must be France over there then," said Chinwag, pointing to a strip of land on the horizon. "Paddle faster, Jimjams."

The two friends paddled towards the land as fast as they could. At last, they pulled their raft out of the sea and flopped on to an empty beach.

"I'm starving," said Jimjams.

"Let's have lunch," said Chinwag. She delved in her soggy duffel bag and pulled out crisps and cake and chocolate bars and cans of fizzy drink. They tucked in hungrily.

# Chapter Three

Just as they were finishing the last crumbs of cake, they heard the most enormous BURP! They turned round to find two fat pirates towering over them.

"I do beg your pardon," said one of the men, who had a plastic parrot tied to his shoulder. "I always do burp when I see food."

"Who are you?" asked Chinwag.

"I'm Cap'n Blowmedown, and this be Cap'n Blessmesoul. If this is not a nosy question, what do you think you're doing on our island?"

"We're looking for my pet rat," said Jimjams.

"It was stolen by Ratnappers," said Chinwag. "Do you mean this isn't France?"

19

"Well blow me down," said Cap'n Blowmedown. "Ratnappers, eh?"

"Well bless me soul," said Cap'n Blessmesoul. "France? Nah. This be Treasure Island. This be where pirates throughout history have buried their treasure."

"Please help us to find Skintail," said Jimjams.

"All right," said Cap'n Blessmesoul. "We're superb at hunting treasure, so rats is going to be easy."

"Have you ever found any treasure?" asked Chinwag.

"Not yet," said Cap'n Blowmedown. "But we be trying very hard."

The two captains lent Jimjams and Chinwag some clothes then set off across the island, on their hands and knees, searching the ground for droppings.

"Is this one?" asked Cap'n Blessmesoul, excitedly.

Chinwag looked. "More like a tortoise dropping," she said.

"Well, bless me soul!" said Cap'n Blessmesoul. "I've never seen a tortoise on our island."

"What about this?" asked Cap'n Blowmedown.

Chinwag looked. "More like a monkey dropping," she said.

"Well, blow me down!" said Cap'n Blowmedown. "I've never seen a monkey on our island."

"Here's one," yelled Jimjams.

"A monkey?" puzzled Cap'n Blowmedown.

"A rat dropping," said Jimjams. "And another, and another."

"Well, bless me soul, that means them there Ratnappers have been on our island without so much as a how do you do!"

They followed the trail of droppings down to the water's edge at the other side of the island – it was only a tiny island – where the pirates' ship, the *Jolly Horrible*, was moored. Cap'n Blessmesoul prepared the dinghy for sailing, and they clambered in.

"Where to?" asked Cap'n Blowmedown.

"Go right," said Jimjams, peering into the water. Cap'n Blowmedown steered left.

"That's left," yelled Chinwag.

"Well blessmesoul," said Cap'n Blessmesoul. "And I've always thought that was right."

"No wonder you've never found any treasure," said Chinwag.

# Chapter Four

A swift wind caught the sail and the *Jolly Horrible* picked up speed. Very soon, Jimjams spotted a speedboat hurtling towards them.

"Watch out!" he screamed. The four sailors threw themselves down on to the floor of the dinghy and felt it swing violently as the speedboat just missed them. They heard a snigger and a snort and a large stone landed in the bottom of the dinghy. It was wrapped in a piece of paper held on by an elastic band. Jimjams picked it up and read:

"YOU ARE OUT OF YOUR DEPTH. GIVE UP AND PAY US THE MONEY. YOUR BEEF-BRAINED PIRATE FRIENDS CAN'T HELP. THEY'LL MAKE A GOOD RAT PIE (JOKE: PIRATE = RAT PIE (ANAGRAM)). SO WILL YOUR RAT."

"Who's he calling beef-brained?" said the pirates together.

"Never mind that," said Jimjams. "It's the Ratnappers! Get after them!"

"Pull down the sail and start rowing," ordered Chinwag.

Chinwag sat at the front of the dinghy and started yelling, "In, out, in, out, faster, out, no slacking, out, don't be lazy, out". The pirates did as they were told – no one argued with Chinwag when she was giving orders – until Jimjams shouted, "We're catching them up! They've stopped to go fishing!"

"What are we going to do when we get there?" asked Cap'n Blowmedown.

"You're going to dive into the water, grab hold of their fishing lines and pull them into the water, while Jimjams and I save Skintail and the other rats."

"That's a great plan you've got there, young lady," said Cap'n Blessmesoul. "Excepting one thing. Me and him can't swim."

"Well now's a good time to learn," said Chinwag.

They let the dinghy drift right up close
to the speedboat, then Jimjams and
Chinwag pushed the two pirates gently
into the water. The pirates doggy paddled
frantically and grabbed the Ratnappers'
fishing lines more to save themselves than
anything else. The Ratnappers fell head
first into the water. While they spluttered

and splashed and struggled and swore,
Jimjams and Chinwag jumped into the
speed boat and hauled their pirate friends

on board. The captains sat at the side going "Grrrr" to the Ratnappers and stamping on their fingers every time they tried to climb in. Jimjams and Chinwag searched the boat, but there was no sign of any rats.

"Where's my rat?" Jimjams screamed at the Ratnappers.

"Shan't tell you," said the Ratnappers.

"Then we'll leave you here," said Chinwag.

"France," cried the
Ratnappers.

"We were right all along,"
said Chinwag. "They must have
laid a false trail of droppings to Treasure
Island."

Jimjams and the pirates tied the dinghy
to the back of the speedboat and two
lifebelts to the back of the dinghy. The
Ratnappers climbed into the lifebelts and
Cap'n Blessmesoul started the engine up.

"Which way?" yelled Chinwag.
"Go left," yelled the Ratnappers.

Cap'n Blessmesoul went left and got it right for the first time in his life.

"Hold tight," he yelled.

Off they went, with the Ratnappers whizzing through the water like a pair of bouncing buoys, screaming directions as they went. And there was France, drawing closer and closer.

"Now no monkey business," said Cap'n Blowmedown to the giddy Ratnappers as they scrambled ashore. "Where next?"

"The Eiffel Tower," said the Ratnappers.

"Taxi!" yelled Chinwag, waving down a passing car and jumping in. "Paris, quick," she commanded in her best French, and then told the Ratnappers, who were squashed breathless between the two pirates, "You can pay".

# Chapter Five

When at last they reached the Eiffel Tower, the pirates had fallen asleep and were lying across the Ratnappers, who couldn't have made a false move if they had wanted to. Jimjams nudged the pirates awake so that the Ratnappers could pay.

"Where now?" said Jimjams to the Ratnappers.

"Second level," said Ratnapper One.

"The lift is full, we'll have to take the stairs," said Chinwag.

"The fatties will never make it," said Ratnapper Two.

"Who are you calling fat?" said Cap'n Blessmesoul. "We be nicely rounded, thanking you."

The Ratnappers pushed their way through the crowds of tourists. By the time they had reached the first level Cap'n Blessmesoul and Cap'n Blowmedown were wheezing and gasping and red in the face like two boiled lobsters.

"We'll just have a little rest here then catch you up," said Cap'n Blowmedown.

"A good idea," said Cap'n Blessmesoul, quickly.

At the second level Jimjams and Chinwag looked around.

"Where's my rat?" asked Jimjams.

"Look above you," said Ratnapper One.

Jimjams and Chinwag stared closely at the mesh of steel girders.

"There!" yelled Jimjams excitedly. "Cages of them! You can hardly see them because of the steelwork."

He turned to ask the Ratnappers how to reach them, but the Ratnappers were just disappearing into the lift that carried people to the top of the tower. They waved cheekily before the doors closed across them.

"I'll call the police while you find Skintail," said Chinwag.

Jimjams looked up again at the cages
high above. The only way to reach them
was to climb the steel girders, and he was
scared of heights. But just then he heard a
heart-rending squeak, a squeak he knew
belonged to Skintail. Skintail was calling
him. Jimjams began to climb.

Crowds gathered below, pointing
excitedly. Jimjams climbed and climbed,
never looking down, until he had almost
reached the middle of the arch. Now he
could see Skintail's pointy nose poking
eagerly through the side of his cage.

"I'm coming, Skintail!" he yelled.

He held on with one hand and leaned across to Skintail's cage. The crowd gasped as he opened the door, grabbed Skintail and put him in his pocket.

"I'll fetch help for you," he shouted to the other rats.

As he began to climb back down, the lift doors opened. The Ratnappers jumped out and headed for the stairs.

"Stop them!" screamed Jimjams, pointing at the two figures.

Just at that moment, the pirates finally made it to Level Two.

"Cor, bless me soul," said Cap'n Blessmesoul. "Them Ratnappers is escaping!"

They hurled themselves at the Ratnappers and flattened them. The crowd cheered. The pirates slapped each

other on the back and helped Jimjams
clamber the rest of the way down. Jimjams
took Skintail from his pocket and held
him up to the crowd.

"There are dozens more up there," he
said.

# Chapter Six

The crowd cheered and some began to climb the steel girders to save the other rats. Chinwag arrived with the police, who immediately carted the Ratnappers off. The Chief Inspector stayed to make an announcement in his best English.

"Jimjams, Chinwag, Cap'n Blessmesoul and Cap'n Blowmedown, it is my greatest pleasure to thank you for solving a crime

that has kept police all over
the world doing overtime
for months. Please accept
this reward for your skill and
bravery." One by one, he hung a
gold medal round their necks. Cap'n
Blessmesoul and Cap'n Blowmedown
couldn't believe their eyes.

"This be treasure, me hearties," said
Cap'n Blessmesoul. "This be the first
treasure we've ever had in our lives."

"It's been a good day's work," said
Chinwag. "It must be worth a Brownie
badge or two."

"I'm just glad to have Skintail back,"
said Jimjams. He pulled him from his
pocket and kissed him on the nose. "He's
worth all the treasure in the world."